All inquiries should be directed to
www.tigerbeanbooks.com

ISBN-13: 979-8-9921787-2-2 - Paperback
ISBN-13: 979-8-9921787-3-9 - Hardcover

Santa Spider and Snowflake Cider

words by
Todd Capps

pictures by
Geta Bell

TIGER
Bean
Book

On a reindeer sleigh-ride to Grandma's house
We come upon a **SANTA SPIDER**

Snuggling with a **TINSEL MOUSE**
Sipping their sweet **SNOWFLAKE CIDER**

With feast prepared and tummies rumbling
We gather to eat but are quite unable

The food is sent flying, dishes tumbling
For someone had spun our new **DREIDEL TABLE!**

I thought it was simply a story untrue
An impossible what, where, and how

'Till I saw it, by moonlight, come wandering through
The mysterious **CHRISTMAS-TREE COW**

With egg-nog in hand we rest tired feet
A holiday evening of cozy delight

Our **GINGERBREAD SOFA** is soft, warm,
and sweet
MACARONI MENORAH lights up the night

CANDY-CANE CATERPILLAR inches along
Toward festivities soon to begin

Past **HOT-COCOA PUDDLES** she carols a song
Careful not to fall in!

I'm sure they are tasty and make a fine treat
But **ELF BERRIES** look far too charming to eat

Another adorable worrisome snack:
POPCORN POLAR BEAR may bite you right back!

She couldn't care less about what we may think
The Holiday Spirit is guiding her way

Whirling and twirling on flippers dressed pink
The **SUGAR PLUM WALRUS** dances ballet

HELP!

With presents to wrap and spiced porridge to cook
We've no time to color the rest of this book!
Do you think you can help us? That sure would be grand!
Our hero you'll be with a crayon in your hand!
(Or marker or pencil...yes, you understand)

SANTA SPIDER

Invented by Todd, drawn by Geta

Colored by _____

DREIDEL TABLE

Invented by Todd, drawn by Geta

Colored by _____

CHRISTMAS-
TREE COW

Colored by _____

Invented by Todd, drawn by Geta

GINGERBREAD SOFA

Colored by _____

Invented by Todd, drawn by Geta

CANDY-CANE CATERPILLAR

Invented by Todd, drawn by Geta

Colored by _____

POPCORN POLAR BEAR

Invented by Todd, drawn by Geta

Colored by _____

SUGAR PLUM WALRUS

Invented by Todd, drawn by Geta

Colored by _____

We hope you enjoyed this Tiger Bean Book! If you would like to receive information on other books in this series, please visit:

tigerbeanbooks.com

Made in the USA
Columbia, SC
17 December 2024